The Teacher
from the
Black Lagoon
and other stories

The Teacher from the Black Lagoon
The Gym Teacher from the Black Lagoon
The Principal from the Black Lagoon
The Librarian from the Black Lagoon

SCHOLASTIC INC.
New York   Toronto   London   Auckland   Sydney
Mexico City   New Delhi   Hong Kong   Buenos Aires

No part of this publication may be reproduced, stored in a retrieval system, or transmitted in any form or by any means, electronic, mechanical, photocopying, recording, or otherwise, without written permission of the publisher. For information regarding permission, write to Scholastic Inc., Attention: Permissions Department, 557 Broadway, New York, NY 10012.

The Teacher from the Black Lagoon
Text copyright © 1989 by Mike Thaler.
Illustrations copyright © 1989 by Jared D. Lee Studio, Inc.

The Gym Teacher from the Black Lagoon
Text copyright © 1994 by Mike Thaler.
Illustrations copyright © 1994 by Jared D. Lee Studio, Inc.

The Principal from the Black Lagoon
Text copyright © 1993 by Mike Thaler.
Illustrations copyright © 1993 by Jared D. Lee Studio, Inc.

The Librarian from the Black Lagoon
Text copyright © 1997 by Mike Thaler.
Illustrations copyright © 1997 by Jared D. Lee Studio, Inc.

All rights reserved. Published by Scholastic Inc.
SCHOLASTIC, CARTWHEEL BOOKS, and associated logos
are trademarks and/or registered trademarks of Scholastic Inc.

ISBN 0-439-84803-2

10 9 8 7 6 5 4 3 2   6 7 8 9 10
Printed in Singapore 46 • This collection first printing, June 2006

The Teacher
from the
Black Lagoon

by Mike Thaler
pictures by Jared Lee

For Dr. Jerry Weiss,
who loves books
and kids
—M.T.

To all my teachers
at the now defunct
Van Buren High School
—J.L.

It's the first day of school.

I wonder who my teacher is.

I hear Mr. Smith has dandruff and warts,

and Mrs. Jones has a whip and a wig.

But Mrs. Green is supposed to be a *real* monster.

Oh my, I have *her*!

Mrs. Green...room 109.

What a bummer!

I sit at a desk.

I fold my hands.

I close my eyes.

I'm too young to die.

Suddenly a shadow covers the door.

It opens....

In slithers Mrs. Green.

She's *really* green!

She has a tail.

She scratches her name on the blackboard—

with her claws!

Freddy Jones throws a spitball.

She curls her lip and breathes fire at him.
Freddy's gone.

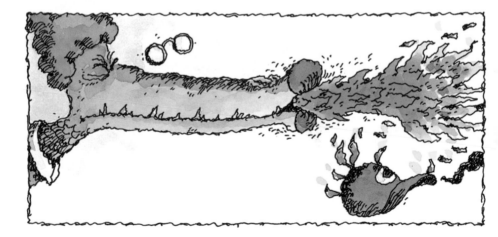

There is just a little pile of ashes on his desk.

"Talk about bad breath," giggles Eric Porter.

She slithers over, unscrews his head,
and puts it on the globe stand.

I bet she gives homework the first day of school.

"Your homework for today," grins Mrs. Green,

smoke rising from her nostrils,

"is pages 1 to 200 in your math book—

all the fraction problems."

"We've never had fractions," shouts Derek Bloom.
"Come up here," she beckons with her claw.

Derek stands by her desk.

"This is a whole boy," she smirks.

She takes a big bite.

"This is half a boy. Now you've had fractions."

Doris Foodle cracks her gum.

Mrs. Green swallows her in one gulp!
"No chewing in class," she smiles.

Mr. Bender, the principal, sticks his head in.

"Keep up the good work,"

he nods and closes the door.

I wish I could get sent to the principal's office.

"Let's call the roll," cackles Mrs. Green.

"Freddy Jones is absent.

Derek Bloom is half here.

Eric Porter is here and there.

Doris Foodle is digesting."

"What about spelling?" shouts Randy Potts.
"Spelling can be *fun*!" beams Mrs. Green,
wiggling her fingers at him.

"Abracadabra Kazam!"

"That's tough to spell," says Randy.

Suddenly there's a flash of light, a puff of smoke, and Randy's a frog.

Penny Weber raises her hand.

"Can I go to the nurse?" she whines.

"What's wrong?" asks Mrs. Green.

"I have a huge headache," says Penny.

Mrs. Green wriggles her fingers.

There's another flash of light,

and Penny's head is the size of a pin.

"Better?" asks Mrs. Green.

"Now it's naptime. Everyone who still has one, put your head on your desk."

I hope I make it to recess.

"Sweet dreams," she cackles as I close my eyes.

Suddenly the bell rings.

I wake up.

There's a pretty woman writing her name
on the blackboard.

She has real skin and no tail.

"I'm Mrs. Green, your teacher," she smiles.

I jump out of my chair, run up,
and hug her.

"Well, thank you," she says,

"I'm glad to be here."

Not as glad as I am!

The Gym Teacher
from the
Black Lagoon

by Mike Thaler
pictures by Jared Lee

*For Alan Boyko,
a friend indeed!*
—M.T.

*To my big brother,
whose first name rhymes with gym.*
—J.L.

We're getting a new gym teacher this year.

He's coming over from the Junior High.

His name is

Mr. Green!

The kids say he's big,

he's mean, and he's rarely seen.

They say he's *very* hairy,

and his knuckles touch the ground.

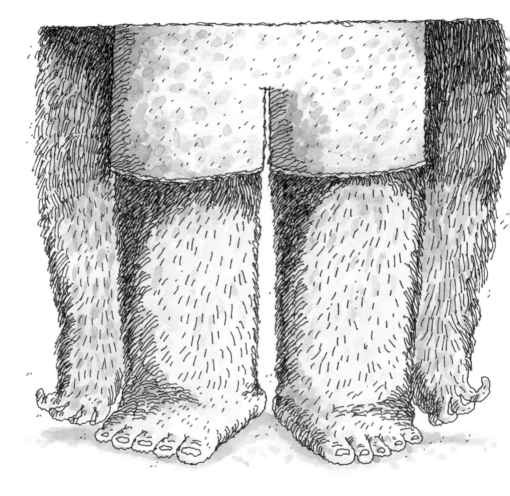

His nickname is COACH KONG and no one has actually heard him speak any words.

He just blows his whistle a lot.

They say he has a little office
full of balls and clubs and tires.

The big kids say he makes you run a lot.
First a lap around the gym.

Then a lap around the school.

Then a lap around the world!

Then he gives you fitness tests.
You have to lift his pickup truck
over your head before the semester ends.
I guess that's why they call it a "pickup" truck.

You spend a lot of time getting in shape.

He makes you do push-ups, pull-ups,

chin-ups, and sit-ups.

But most of the kids just do *throw-ups.*

Then you have to climb THE ROPE.
If you don't reach the top, he sets
the bottom on fire!

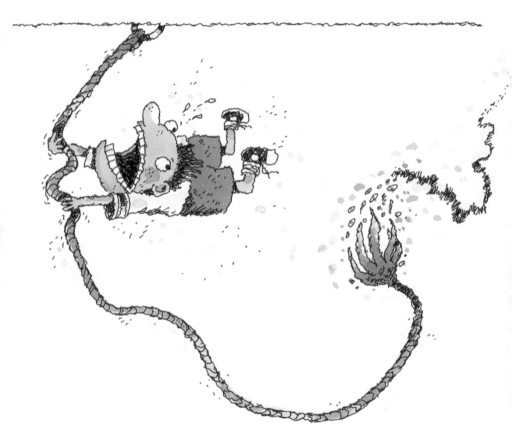

They say there are still kids up in the ceiling
of the Junior High gym.

If you don't pass the fitness tests,
your body is *donated* to science.

Then there's the posture test.

If you don't pass that, he ties you

between two boards.

But there are games, too.

He makes you play DODGE ball…

with his truck!

And TAG with Crazy Glue…

And baseball with real bats!

Then there's THE PARACHUTE!
He has us all hold on tight to the side
and jump out of an airplane.

He's also big on gymnastics.

He makes you walk "the beam"

and jump over "the horse."

He makes you do

HANDSTANDS,

HEADSTANDS,

NOSE STANDS,

and MUSIC STANDS.

He makes you do SOMERSAULTS

and CARTWHEELS.

But the worst thing is SQUARE DANCING…
with the *girls*!

Oh, oh! There's his whistle!
I better go line up.

"Hi, kids. I'm Mr. Green, your new gym teacher."

I can't believe it!

He's a regular guy!

"Let's play some basketball," says Mr. Green.
We do, and I score two baskets.

This is great!

I'm going to like gym.

The Principal
from the
Black Lagoon

by Mike Thaler
pictures by Jared Lee

For Bill Rich
and all principals
who love kids.
—M.T.

For Dad,
who always encouraged
this kid to draw.
—J.L.

It's the third day of school.

I've been sent to the principal's office.

What a bummer!

I hear the principal, Mrs. Green, is a real monster.

Kids go to her office and never come back.

The waiting room is supposed to be filled with bones and skeletons.

Doris Foodle was sent there for chewing gum.

They say her skeleton still has a bubble
in its mouth.

I walk in.
I take a seat.
The rug is red.
That's so the blood
won't show.

I hear she uses tall kids as coat racks.

The short kids she feeds to her pet alligator.

The fat ones she uses as paperweights.

The thin ones she uses as bookmarks.

I'm too young to be a bookmark!

Then there's her twelve-foot paddle.
It's supposed to have poisoned spikes on it.

If you're lucky you can get put in "the cages."
She has them under her desk.

If you're *really* lucky you get sent home in chains.

But most kids she keeps for her *experiments*.

Derek Bloom was sent here yesterday.

They say he wound up with the head of a dog.

They say Freddy Jones has the feet of a chicken,

and Eric Porter, the hands of a hamster.

I'm too good-looking to have the ears of a rabbit!

All I did was snatch Mrs. Jones's wig.

It's very quiet today.

Usually, they say, there's a lot of screaming.

Maybe she's in a good mood.

Even if I survive, this will affect my whole life.

In the future I'll be running for president.
I'll be ahead in the polls.

And then it will come out!

I can see the headlines...

Oh-oh, there's a shadow at the glass.

Now I'm in the *jaws of fate.*

The door slowly opens.

There's a pretty woman standing there.
She's a master of disguise.

"Come in, Hubie."

I go in.

She closes the door behind me.

I look around.

There's only the coat rack.

It doesn't look like anyone I know.

I look around for the alligator.

There's only a turtle.

It looks a little like Randy Potts.

"Now," says Mrs. Green. "Are we having a little trouble in class?"

"Well," says I, "I was sweeping up the room and by accident Mrs. Jones's wig got caught on the broom handle."

"Well, we'll have to apologize, won't we?"

"Yes, we will."

"And the next time, *we'll* have to be more careful."

"Yes, we will! Yes, we will!"

"Now run along."

"Is that *all*???"

"Close the door."

Boy, was I lucky.

Those flowers on her desk were probably poisonous.

Just one whiff and you would turn purple and die.

Fortunately I held my breath.

I went into her cave and I have returned without the ears of a rabbit.

I'll have to sweep *her* office sometime and see if *she* wears a wig!

The Librarian
from the
Black Lagoon

by Mike Thaler
pictures by Jared Lee

For Jared D. Lee,
Friend, partner, genius
—M.T.

To the nice people who work at the
Public Library in Lebanon, Ohio
—J.L.

Today our class is going to the library.
We've been hearing some really scary things
about that place.

The library is somewhere behind the boiler room.
It's called "MEDIA CENTER OF THE EARTH."

Mrs. Beamster is the librarian.
The kids call her "THE LAMINATOR."

They say she laminates you
if you talk in the library.

She also has a library assistant named IGOR.

You know you're getting close to the library by the signs on the wall.

They say you're allowed to stay in the library
as long as you can hold your breath.
Some kids last as long as a minute.

That doesn't include the time in
the *DECONTAMINATION ROOM.*

There you put on hair nets and rubber gloves.

Next, you have to go through the
GUM DETECTOR!

Once you're finally in the library, you can't actually check out books.

In fact, you can't take them off the shelves.

To keep the books in alphabetical order, Mrs. Beamster bolts them together.

Also, they say, the shelves are electrified.

If you twist your neck and squint,

you can read the spines.

Everyone says the best part of a
library visit is *STORYTIME*.
All the kids stand at attention while
Mrs. Beamster reads one of
the cards from the card catalog.

Or, if you catch her in a good mood, she'll recite the Dewey decimal system by heart.

They say Mrs. Beamster has a crush on Mr. Dewey
and that she carries his picture in a lead locket
around her neck.

She also has rubber stamps on the soles of her shoes.
And, whenever she steps… it says *OVERDUE!*

She seems to have ears on the back of her head.

If she catches you whispering…

YOU'RE *LAMINATED!*

They say she puts glue on all the chairs
so you won't WRIGGLE.

Then she shows you slides of all her vacations since 1902.

She goes to the same place every year—the Library of Congress.

Mrs. Beamster also subscribes to three magazines: *The Morticians Monthly*, *The Complete Pamphlet of Zip Codes*, and *Spots Illustrated: The Magazine for Cleaner Laundry*.

These you *DO* get to read.

But stay away from her plants.

They are VENUS FLY TRAPS!

And don't pet the animals in her petting zoo, which contains a PIRANHA and a PORCUPINE.

Don't go near her computer either,
it uses a *real* MOUSE!

Well, it's time to go.

As we get near the library there are lots of signs.

We march right in and sit down in little chairs.
These must be the ones without glue.
Mrs. Beamster comes over with an armful of books
and puts them on our table.

Then she smiles and hands me one.

It's a book of KNOCK-KNOCK JOKES!

I'm going to love the library!